ENJOY MORE ADVENTURES WiTH
JASMINE TOGUCHI

Jasmine Toguchi, Mochi Queen

Jasmine Toguchi, Super Sleuth

PRAISE FOR
JASMINE TOGUCHI, MOCHI QUEEN

A JUNIOR LIBRARY GUILD SELECTION
AN AMAZON.COM BEST BOOK OF THE YEAR
A CHICAGO PUBLIC LIBRARY BEST OF THE BEST BOOKS

"In this new early chapter book series, Florence introduces readers to a bright character who is grappling with respecting authority while also forging her own path. Vuković's illustrations are expressive and imbue Jasmine and the Toguchi family with sweetness . . . **This first entry nicely balances humor with the challenges of growing up; readers will devour it.**"

—*School Library Journal*

"[A]n **adorable and heartwarming** story about a kid who wants to feel special and do something first for once, along with a nice overview of a Japanese New Year celebration."

—*Booklist*

"Florence . . . warmly traces Jasmine's efforts to get strong (and fast), her clashes and tender moments with her family, and the ins and outs of making mochi . . . **[The] spot illustrations evoke Japanese Sumi-e painting while playfully capturing Jasmine's willfulness and her family's closeness.**"

—*Publishers Weekly*

"Florence paints **a lovely picture of a warm, extended family** whose members truly care about one another and take each other seriously . . . **New readers thirsty for series fiction will look forward to more stories about Jasmine and her family.**"

—*Kirkus Reviews*

MINEGUCHI

DRUMMER
GiRL

DEBBi MiCHiKO FLORENCE   PiCTURES BY ELiZABET VUKOVIĆ

FARRAR STRAUS GIROUX • NEW YORK

Farrar Straus Giroux Books for Young Readers

An imprint of Macmillan Publishing Group, LLC

175 Fifth Avenue, New York, NY 10010

Text copyright © 2018 by Debbi Michiko Florence

Illustrations copyright © 2018 by Elizabet Vuković

All rights reserved

Printed in the United States of America by LSC Communications,

Harrisonburg, Virginia

Designed by Kristie Radwilowicz

First edition, 2018

Hardcover: 10 9 8 7 6 5 4 3 2 1

Paperback: 10 9 8 7 6 5 4 3 2 1

mackids.com

Library of Congress Control Number: 2017944538

Hardcover ISBN: 9780374304164

Paperback ISBN: 9780374308360

Our books may be purchased in bulk for promotional, educational, or

business use. Please contact your local bookseller or the Macmillan

Corporate and Premium Sales Department at (800) 221-7945

ext. 5442 or by e-mail at MacmillanSpecialMarkets@macmillan.com.

CONTENTS

CONTENTS

AN EXCITING ANNOUNCEMENT

Bong bong bong bing!

Ms. Sanchez, my third-grade teacher, played the start-of-the-day song on her xylophone. Everyone in room 5, including me, sat up straight at their desk and got quiet.

"Happy Monday, class," Ms. Sanchez said. "Buenos días!"

That means good morning. Ms. Sanchez was teaching us Spanish.

"Buenos días, Señora Sanchez," I said along with my classmates.

"We have a special guest this morning," she said.

Just then, Mrs. Tasker, our principal, walked into the room. Even though we were already sitting up straight, we all sat up a little straighter. The principal is like the boss of the school. If a student gets into trouble, he or she gets sent to the principal's office.

I, Jasmine Toguchi, try hard to stay out of trouble. But sometimes trouble finds me. That's what my mom says, at least. I like to climb my neighbor's apricot tree, play dress up with my best friend, Linnie Green, make collages, and eat brownies without nuts. Sometimes I tear my jeans while climbing, lose track of time, get glue on the table, and leave crumbs on the floor. All things my mom wishes I wouldn't do.

"Good morning," Mrs. Tasker said.

"Good morning, Mrs. Tasker," I said with the rest of the class.

She had a stack of papers in her hand. Was she giving us homework? I glanced at Ms. Sanchez for a clue. She was smiling. It couldn't be a bad thing if she was smiling. Then again, she smiled when she gave us homework. She had a strange sense of what was fun.

"I have an exciting announcement," Mrs. Tasker said. "This Saturday, we're having a school-wide talent show. All of your families will be invited."

Tommy Fraser raised his hand from the front row. "What's a talent show?" he blurted out without waiting to be called on.

"I'm glad you asked, Tommy," Mrs. Tasker said. "A talent show is when students can show off a special

DRAKE
ELEMENTARY
SCHOOL

TALENT SHOW!
Saturday Night

Name: _____

Talent: _____

Parent signature: _____

or fun talent. Like singing, or playing an instrument, or reciting a poem you wrote. Anything, really! You can choose to do something on your own, with a group, or with the entire class. I'll let Ms. Sanchez help you make that decision."

Linnie and I smiled at each other.

"Put on your thinking caps," Mrs. Tasker said. "Fill out the form with your special talent and get a parent to sign it. The show will be in the auditorium on Saturday night."

Wowee zowee! This sounded like fun! I had many talents. Which one would I choose to perform for the talent show?

LUNCH BREAK

After Mrs. Tasker left, Ms. Sanchez began the math lesson. I was so excited I couldn't keep the numbers in my head. At least not in the way Ms. Sanchez wanted.

Ms. Sanchez wrote the number 4 on the board. I thought about four things I could do for my talent: pound mochi, make a collage, read from my favorite book, or make up a silly dance. I looked over at Daisy Wang. She took ballet lessons. Okay, so maybe I wouldn't dance.

After our math lesson, Ms. Sanchez said, "Let's review this week's vocabulary words. Choose three words from the list and write a sentence for each one. Use your very best handwriting."

I stared at my vocabulary list.

- **ability:** the skill to do something
- **celebration:** a joyous ceremony or gathering
- **journey:** a long trip
- **pause:** to stop for a short time before going on
- **wisdom:** knowledge and good sense

I chose three words, thought of sentences, and wrote them down:

I have the ability to do many things in the talent show.

I will pause in my schoolwork to think of what I can do in the talent show.

I have the wisdom to decide on my best talent.

The morning took forever to go by. I couldn't wait to talk with my friends about the talent show. When lunchtime finally came, I sat with Linnie, Tommy, and Daisy, like I did every lunch.

Linnie opened her green unicorn lunch box and took out a peanut butter and peach jam sandwich, carrot sticks, and a juice box. She handed me her yogurt and I gave her my banana. I used to bring sandwiches every day, but when my grandma visited from Japan, she made omusubi. I loved eating the rice balls wrapped in nori, or seaweed. Now whenever we have leftover rice from dinner, Mom makes omusubi for my lunch the next day. Sometimes Mom puts a treat in the middle of my rice ball, like pickled radish or a piece of roast chicken.

Tommy unpacked his usual lunch of a turkey sandwich on wheat bread, potato chips, and an apple. We all turned to Daisy. Her mother was a baker, so Daisy brought the best desserts, and she always shared. Today, she had star-shaped cookies dusted with powdered sugar.

"I can make cookies like that," Maggie

Milsap said from the table next to ours. Maggie moved here to Los Angeles from Portland, Oregon, at the beginning of third grade. She didn't know anyone at Drake Elementary. Ms. Sanchez said to be friendly with Maggie to make her feel welcome, but sometimes it was hard. Especially when she bragged a lot.

"What are you going to do for the talent show?" I asked my friends. Ms. Sanchez had the class vote after our math lesson, and we had chosen to do individual talents.

"I'm going to play the piano," Linnie said. "Ms. Sanchez said I can play the piano that Mr. Peters uses for music class."

"You'll be wonderful," I said. Linnie has been playing since she was five. She's very good.

"I'm going to show off my yo-yo skills," Tommy said. "I can do three tricks with my yo-yo."

"That sounds amazing," I said. I turned to Daisy. "Will you dance?"

She nodded. "I'll ask my ballet teacher. I'm sure she can help me plan a short dance for the show."

Maggie Milsap leaned over from her table.

"I'm going to play the violin," she said, even though none of us had asked her. "My teacher says I'm a natural talent."

"What are you going to do, Jasmine?" Linnie asked.

"I am having a hard time choosing one of my talents," I said. "Maybe I will make a collage."

"I can make great collages," Maggie said. "But playing the violin will probably be more interesting for the audience."

I thought about my friends. Their talents were perfect for sharing onstage. I tried to imagine making a collage onstage, sitting at a table and cutting out pictures and words from magazines and gluing them onto cardboard. That might not be very interesting.

I couldn't bring Mrs. Reese's apricot tree to school and show off my climbing skills. I was very good at pounding mochi, but that took a long time and Ms. Sanchez said that we each had only two minutes to perform.

"At my old school, I was the best at many things," Maggie said. "I'm going to be the best at the talent show, too!"

"It's not a contest," I said.

"I'll bet it is," Maggie said. "I'll bet Mrs. Tasker is going to judge us and pick who is the very best. My daddy says, 'Life is a competition.'"

I imagined Maggie standing onstage with a huge trophy.

Suddenly the talent show didn't seem as fun

as I thought it would be. Everyone had a perfect talent except for me!

Walnuts!

By the end of lunchtime, my head was full
of worries.

WHAT TO DO?

After lunch, we had silent-reading time. I opened my favorite book, *Charlotte's Web*, but I couldn't concentrate. I was at one of the best parts of the book: when Charlotte the spider comes up with a plan to save her best friend, Wilbur the pig. I wished my best friend, Linnie, could come up with a plan to save me from the show. But she didn't even know that I didn't have a talent, and I was too embarrassed to tell her.

The rest of the school day dragged on. Finally I heard a happy sound.

Bing bong bong bing!

Ms. Sanchez was playing the end-of-the-day song on her xylophone. That gave me an idea. As everyone got their backpack and coat from the closet, I went up to Ms. Sanchez.

"Do you think I can learn to play the xylophone in time for the talent show?" I asked.

Ms. Sanchez nodded. "I'm sure you can. Is that what you would like to do?"

"May I try?"

She handed me her special xylophone mallet. Nobody in class was allowed to touch it.

I hit the xylophone.

Bong bong BONK clooong CLINK bong bing.

"What is that awful noise?" Maggie Milsap asked, poking her head out of the closet.

I handed the mallet back to Ms. Sanchez. "I guess I don't have talent on the xylophone."

"It just takes a little practice," Ms. Sanchez said. "I can show you a tune to play."

"I don't need to practice the violin," Maggie said. "I'm already great."

"It's okay," I said to Ms. Sanchez. "I have other big talents, but I wanted to see what the xylophone felt like. I will surprise all of you with my talent!"

"I'm looking forward to seeing what it is," Ms. Sanchez said. "Now, class, let's go out to our meeting spot. It's almost time for dismissal."

As we stood by the tree, waiting to be picked up, Linnie came over to me. "I'm so happy you figured out what to do for the show," she said. "What is your talent?"

"It's a surprise," I said. That was the truth. It was going to be a surprise for me, too, since I had no clue what my talent would be. Everyone else knew what to do. I wasn't ready to admit that I didn't know yet. Even to my best friend.

"My parents always give me a prize for being the best," Maggie said, standing close to me. "At my old school, I always got perfect scores on my tests and homework. When I win the talent show, my parents will probably take me to a fancy restaurant for dinner."

I had nothing to say to Maggie Milsap.

I was glad Mom showed up right then to walk me and my big sister, Sophie, home. I didn't want to listen to Maggie anymore. She was making me feel bad.

"Guess what?" Sophie said to Mom. "We're having a school talent show on Saturday and you and Dad are invited to watch us!"

"We'll be sure to be there," Mom said.

"What are you going to do?" I asked Sophie.

"We're doing a class play," Sophie said. "We've already been practicing, so it's a great way to show off our talents!"

"How exciting," Mom said.

"I need a costume," Sophie said. "I'm the queen."

That was the perfect part for my sister, actually. She was super-bossy.

"I'll bet Mrs. Reese has something you can wear," Mom said.

Mrs. Reese was our neighbor and my friend who lived two houses down. She was older than my mom and dad, but she listened to me, made me brownies with no nuts, and let me climb her tree. Best of all, her garage was full of costumes. Linnie and I played dress up in there.

Mom squeezed my hand. "What will you do, Jasmine?"

"I haven't decided yet," I said.

When we got home, I went to my room and pulled out a flat box from under my bed. I couldn't do a collage onstage, but maybe I could get an idea from some I had already made. One by one, I took out my collages.

In the middle of the stack was a collage of my favorite animal—the flamingo. I wished I had a pet flamingo! If I had one, I could take it with me to the talent show and have it do tricks, like stand on one leg for a long time. Flamingos are very good at that. Maybe I could pretend to be a flamingo. I thought about standing on the stage and balancing on one leg. I shook my head. That would be fun, but was probably not a talent. *What was a talent anyway?*

By the time Mom called us for dinner, my stomach was in knots.

Dad passed me the green beans. I am not a fan of green beans. I took a very small scoop.

"You haven't filled out your form yet, Jasmine," Mom said.

"Mine is going to be a surprise," I said, taking a big bite of green beans. Mom has a lot of rules and one of them is no talking with your mouth full. If I kept my mouth full during dinner, I wouldn't have to admit that I didn't have any talent.

I needed to figure it out, and fast!

STiCKS

After dinner, Sophie practiced her lines for the play with Dad. I was afraid Mom would ask me again what I was planning to do for the show. I thought about walking to Mrs. Reese's house to climb my thinking tree, but I wanted to go somewhere nobody would find me and ask me questions about my talent. So I went to our garage.

Our garage was not as interesting as Mrs. Reese's. Hers had boxes full of fun costumes.

We had a lot of boxes, but most of them had boring things in them, such as Mom's old files and Dad's textbooks. Mrs. Reese had a special door around the side, like a little house. Ours had a regular garage door that we left open during the day when we were home.

I plopped down in an old stuffed chair in the garage. Dust puffed up in a cloud, tickling my nose.

Dad kept his woodworking tools in the garage. He liked to build things like bookcases and tables. Maybe that was Dad's talent. Dad was a history teacher at a college. That was his job.

Mom's job was being an editor. She worked with writers, fixing their mistakes. Mom had a lot of talents, like making up rules and sniffing out trouble. She was also good at needlepoint. She made pretty pictures using a needle and thread. It looked like a lot of work, but she said it was fun.

Sophie wrote poems and now she was an actress. She also played on a soccer team. She had lots of talents. That didn't seem fair. Maybe that was why I didn't have a talent, because everyone in my family had used them all up. There was no talent left over for me.

"There you are," Mom said, standing in front of the garage.

I guess it wasn't a very good hiding place after all.

Mom sat down on the arm of the chair and put her hand on my shoulder. "Is something wrong? You didn't ask for any dessert tonight."

Like I said, Mom was good at sniffing out trouble. And I had trouble with a capital *T*.

"Are you having a hard time figuring out what to do in the talent show?" she asked.

"How did you know?" I asked.

"A mom knows," she said. "Is there a way I can help you?"

"I don't have a talent," I said, slouching in the chair. "Linnie plays the piano. Sophie is an actress."

"I'm sure you have a talent. What are some things you like to do?"

"I like to climb trees, make collages, and pound mochi. But those are not things I can do for the talent show," I said.

"Hmmm. Why do you like doing those things?" Mom asked.

I leaned my head back and thought. "Climbing makes me feel free like a bird," I said. "And pounding mochi makes me feel strong. Creating my own collages makes me happy."

"All good things!" Mom said with a smile. "In fact, that reminds me of something . . ." She walked to the back of the garage and started rummaging around.

I turned in the chair, peering up over the back of it. Mom pushed boxes out of the way. She opened one and then another, digging through each of them. Mom was making a mess. That was not like Mom at all.

"Aha!" Mom shouted. She turned around and raised two fat wooden sticks.

I didn't understand why she was so excited over sticks.

"This is what you can do for your talent," Mom said, waving them in the air.

"You want me to wave sticks on the stage?" That didn't sound like a good talent at all.

"No," Mom said, laughing. *"Taiko!"*

"What-ko?"

"It's a special Japanese drum," Mom said. "I used to play it in college. It made me feel all the things you mentioned. Playing taiko made me feel free and strong and happy."

She handed me the sticks. They reminded me of chopsticks, but were much bigger and fatter. They were heavier than chopsticks, too. I gripped them and sucked on my bottom lip. I remembered what it had felt like hitting Ms. Sanchez's xylophone. It was not good.

"That's not your usual look," Mom said, patting my arm. "I need to make a phone call, but I think tomorrow you and I are going to go somewhere special."

"Really? Just you and me? No Sophie?"

"Nope! Sophie's going to Maya's house,"

Mom said. "I think you'll enjoy our little outing."

Suddenly I didn't care so much about the talent show. I hardly ever got time with Mom without Sophie. I couldn't wait till tomorrow after school!

AFTER-SCHOOL SURPRISE

The next day, Ms. Sanchez collected the forms that listed everyone's talent. When she got to me, I told her I would give her my paper tomorrow.

"That's fine," Ms. Sanchez said. "As long as I have it before dress rehearsal on Friday."

"What's a dress rehearsal?" Tommy asked.

"A dress rehearsal is a way to practice for the actual show. The entire school will go through a dress rehearsal on Friday to prepare for Saturday," Ms. Sanchez said. "And this way, the rest of the school can also enjoy the show."

"It's like we'll have *two* talent shows!" Maggie said.

"Yes," Ms. Sanchez said. "One for the school as practice, and one for the parents on Saturday. Isn't this exciting?"

Walnuts! I had even less time to come up with a talent than I thought. I had to be ready by Friday. That was just three days away! I needed a miracle. A miracle is when something amazing happens right when you don't expect it.

At lunch, Tommy took out his blue-and-yellow yo-yo from his lunch bag.

"Watch how the colors change," he said. The yo-yo flashed up and down, turning green as the colors spun fast.

Daisy stood up on her toes and danced around the lunch table, looking like a pretty butterfly flitting on a breeze.

Linnie moved her hands on the tabletop, her fingers flying up and down the imaginary keyboard.

At the next table, Maggie Milsap talked loudly. This wasn't anything new, because she always spoke loudly. "I played my violin piece perfectly yesterday. My teacher said I'm gifted. I don't even need to practice! I'll definitely win first prize Saturday night."

Everyone had a talent except me. I thought about Mom's special sticks. I didn't know where she was taking me after school, but it was definitely going to be better than sitting around surrounded by talent.

＊ ＊ ＊

Mom was waiting for me after school. I slid into the backseat of our car and put on my seat belt. I was excited to hang out with her. And maybe, just maybe, I would discover what my talent was!

"Where are we going?" I asked quickly.

"When I played taiko in college," Mom said, "I belonged to a group of taiko players. One of the other players just moved back to Los Angeles. She says she'll be happy to teach you a song you can play in your show."

"Wowee zowee! That's fantastic!" Good thing I had a seat belt on, because I was so excited, I almost bounced out of my seat.

Mom drove through a gate that said BEACH WALK. We curved around the little street past tan town houses until Mom pulled into a driveway. When we walked up to the door, we didn't even need to press the doorbell. The door swung open and a woman with long brown hair and a big smile flew out and hugged my mom.

"Sandra!" the woman squealed. "It's been forever!"

Mom grinned. "It's great to see you!"

The lady turned to me and smiled. "You must be Jasmine."

I nodded. It was weird to see my mom with a friend, all hugging and grinning.

"You can call me Kat," she said.

She turned back to Mom. Kat reminded me of a hummingbird. She was fluttery and quick. "Come on in."

I followed Mom and Kat into the living room. Inside, there were two funny-looking drums. They were not like any drums I had ever seen. One drum was shaped like a barrel and sat on a low stand. The other one was smaller, like a slice had been taken off

  the big drum and put on a higher wooden stand. Black dots circled the rims of the drums.

"Taiko," Kat said, facing me, "is the Japanese word for drum. There are a lot of different kinds of taiko. This one"—she pointed to the barrel-shaped drum—"is called nagado-daiko. The smaller one is called hira-daiko."

"Cool," I said. I couldn't wait to play. I reached out to touch the big one.

Kat held up her hand just as Mom grasped my arm, holding me back. "There are rules to taiko."

I sighed. Of course there were rules. There were always rules.

THE RULES

"First rule," Kat said, smiling at me. "We respect the drum. We don't touch it, or lean on it, or put things on top of it."

"If we can't touch it," I said, "how do we play it?"

"Good question!" Kat said. "We use bachi, or sticks."

She picked up two sticks like the ones Mom had at home. She handed them to me.

"The first thing you need to learn is how to

hold your bachi at rest." Kat took another pair of sticks and held them in her left hand, down at her side. And she stood with her legs together. I copied her.

"Good job, Jasmine," Mom said.

Her words filled me with a bubble of joy.

"Okay, come stand in front of the hiradaiko," Kat said as she moved to the bigger barrel drum. "Now I'll teach you the ready position."

She jumped her legs apart and held the sticks just above the center of the drum. I copied her again, holding my sticks over the smaller drum.

"Excellent!" Kat said. "Let's practice."

She had me go from rest to

ready three times. It reminded me of doing jumping jacks in school. *Wowee zowee!* I was a natural!

"Can we play now?" I asked.

Kat laughed. Her laugh was low, like a cat's purr. "Okay, we're going to hit the drum once. Raise your right arm high, like this, but don't bend your arm backward behind your shoulder."

I copied her. She nodded and gave me a big smile. I glanced at Mom and she was smiling, too.

"After I say ichi, ni, san, SO-RE," Kat said, "strike the drum hard. I'll show you.

"Ichi, ni, san, SO-RE," Kat said in a strong voice. She raised her right stick and brought it down on her drum, making a big booming sound.

"Awesome!" I said.

"Do you know what the words mean?" Mom asked me.

"Well, ichi is one, ni is two, and san is three," I said. I knew some Japanese words, even though I couldn't speak the language really well like Mom and Dad. "But I'm not sure about SO-RE."

"It's called a kiai and it doesn't mean anything. It's a gathering of your energy with your voice that comes from your center," Kat said. "Are you ready?"

I nodded, holding my sticks over the drum and standing with my legs apart.

"Ichi, ni, san, SO-RE!" Kat said.

I lifted my right arm and hit the drum, hard.

BOOM!

"Whoa!" I stared at the drum and then at my arm. It was like the sound

went from the drum, up the stick, and through my whole body. It made me feel strong! This was the perfect talent for me. Not only did it make me feel strong, it also made me feel happy.

Plus, it was easy! I was gifted, like Maggie's teacher said she was.

A buzzing came from Kat's pocket. She pulled out her phone and looked at the screen.

"My son's soccer game was canceled. I have to go and pick him up," she said. "I'm so sorry. Let's continue the lesson tomorrow."

Tomorrow? That would only give me

two days before the dress rehearsal. Then again, I was pretty great already, so maybe I wouldn't need to practice much.

I smiled. Finally I had my talent! I got my miracle!

TAIKO

On Wednesday during lunch, everyone was busy practicing their talents. Linnie played her pretend piano on the lunch table, Tommy spun his yo-yo, and Daisy danced around us.

Maggie Milsap walked over to our table.

"I don't need to practice," she said. "My violin piece is perfect. My teacher said so."

"Well, *my* teacher told me I was excellent," I said.

Tommy's yo-yo stopped in mid-flight,

swinging around his arm and hanging from the string. Daisy leaped over to me, and Linnie stopped playing the table.

"What teacher?" Linnie asked.

"My taiko teacher!" I grinned.

"Is that a word?" Maggie said.

"It's Japanese for drum," I said, "and it's a special drum. I'm going to play it for my talent."

"That's fab, Jasmine," Linnie said, clapping her hands.

"Wow!" Tommy said. "Drums are cool!"

"I can't wait to hear you play," Daisy said, doing a ballet twirl.

"I'm going to win that first-place prize," I said.

"I don't think Ms. Sanchez said it was a contest," Daisy said.

"Doesn't matter," Maggie said as she walked away. "*I'm* going to be the best. I always am."

Linnie patted my shoulder. "Don't let her get to you, Jasmine," she said.

I couldn't wait to get to my next taiko lesson!

* * *

"I have to run some errands," Mom said as she pulled up in front of Kat's house. "Will you be okay by yourself?"

"Hai!" I said the Japanese word for yes and

held up my taiko sticks, the bachi that Mom had given me.

"Have fun," she said. Her smile turned into her serious face. "And behave yourself."

"Of course," I said.

Kat was waiting for me with the same two drums in the room. I greeted her with a bow and said, "Konnichiwa." That meant good afternoon.

Kat smiled and bowed back to me. "Konnichiwa, Jasmine. Are you ready to learn your song?"

"Hai!"

"I love your enthusiasm," Kat said.

We practiced the rest and ready positions.

"Great job, Jasmine!" Kat said. "You have a good memory. Ready?"

Then, without any warning, she said, "Ichi, ni, san, SO-RE!"

I lifted my right arm with Kat, and we both hit our drums at the same time.

BOOM!

The sound was louder and stronger when we both played together.

"Very good! Now we're going to play a game called Copy Kat," she said, her eyes bright and smiling. "Get it? Copy Kat!"

I got it and I laughed with her, even if her joke was silly.

"I'll hit the drum, and you copy exactly what I do," Kat said.

Kat hit the drum four times. Her arms flew up and down—right, left, right, left. I copied her.

Boom, boom, boom, boom!

Then she hit the drum four times faster, and I copied her.

Boomboomboomboom!

She hit the drum three times and then on the fourth hit, she struck the side.

Boom, boom, boom, clack.

Over and over, she hit the drum and I copied her. She got fancy and spun in a circle before the last strike. I copied her. My forehead got sweaty and I was having a hard time breathing, like when I run around the track at school. I gasped for breath. Then Kat stopped.

I stopped, too. My outsides were all sweaty, but my insides were all happy.

"Very good, Jasmine," Kat said. "Are you ready to learn your song?"

I nodded so hard it was like my head would fall off. My hair stuck to my face with sweat.

This was it! I was going to be a perfect taiko player for the talent show.

A LOT OF WORRIES

"First we're going to learn the sequence before you play the song. You have a good memory, so I think it will come easy to you," Kat said. "It's 5, 5, 8, 5, 3, 3, 5, big 8."

My eyes went wide. That was a lot of numbers! And they didn't make sense like when Ms. Sanchez taught math. In math class, 5 plus 5 equals 10. But these were just a bunch of mixed-up numbers.

"It's okay," Kat said. "Let's break it down."

She went over the numbers in sections and I repeated them until I did finally remember them.

"See?" Kat said. "You're doing great!"

I grinned.

"This is what the numbers mean," Kat said. "Five means you hit the drum five times and then lift both arms and say HA! Eight means you hit it eight times and then swing your arms down by your side and up over your head and say SO-RE! Three, you hit the drum three times."

My eyes got big again. That was a lot to remember!

"For the last eight, called Big Eight, you hit the drum slower eight times and then you yell SAH and make up a pose of your own and hold it," Kat said. She held her arms straight up and yelled, "SAH!"

I smiled. Being able to make up my pose sounded like fun.

"Let's try it," Kat said, "without hitting the drum."

We practiced on air drums and after a few times, it wasn't so hard to remember anymore. I was definitely talented at taiko! And I was definitely going to win first prize!

"Let's try it on the taiko," Kat said.

"YAY!" I shouted.

Kat stood in front of the big drum and I stood in front of the smaller one. I stood at rest like she did until she said, "Ready!" and we both jumped into ready position.

"Ichi, ni, san, SO-RE," Kat said.

I lifted my arm and my stick flew out of my

hand. I watched in horror as it clunked onto the ground.

Kat leaned over, picked it up, and handed it back to me. "It's okay, Jasmine. Just remember to keep a good grip on your bachi. But not too tight! Let's try again. Just the first count of five."

This time my sticks stayed in my hands, but I forgot to yell HA and lift my hands at the end of the five hits.

We practiced and practiced. I dropped my sticks three times. I messed up the order. I forgot to yell HA. Maybe I wasn't so talented after all.

We kept playing the song over and over, and I kept goofing up. My arms felt rubbery and my hands started to hurt, but I kept going. Finally I did the whole song without any mistakes. My smile was so big it hurt my cheeks.

"Fantastic, Jasmine," Kat said, smiling, too.

Mom walked in and said, "I heard that, Jasmine. You sounded pretty good."

"Thanks!"

"Jasmine did great," Kat said. "She just needs to keep practicing."

Kat thought I had to practice more. I sucked on my lip. I was not naturally talented.

"Also," Kat said to Mom, "I can't bring the hira-daiko until Saturday at the show. I need the drums Saturday morning."

Oh no! I thought I'd get to take it home. How would I practice without the drum?

"We'll set up a gomi-kan for Jasmine to practice on at home," Mom said.

I had no idea what that was, but it probably wasn't a hira-daiko like I'd been playing.

"Can you give us a short demo?" Mom asked Kat. "It's been a while since I've seen a taiko performance."

"Sure," Kat said.

Kat was a whirling, swirling, taiko-drumming superstar. She hit the drum and spun her sticks. She shouted and bounced and jumped and played the most amazing song ever.

This made me worry. My song was shorter and not as flashy as Kat's. She didn't make any mistakes. I wished I could play like her. I wasn't even sure I could play my *own* song without mistakes. And how was I going to practice without a drum? I kept thinking about Maggie and how perfect she was. She didn't need to practice. Even Linnie, Daisy, and Tommy were already good at their talents.

What was I going to do?

SOPHIE'S ADVICE

Thursday was Mrs. Peepers day, the worst day of the week. Mom worked at home on Mondays and Fridays, and at the office on Tuesdays and Wednesdays, but only until it was time to pick us up at school. On Thursdays, Mom worked all day at the office and Dad taught classes and met with students at the college. So that meant Mrs. Peepers, our babysitter, picked up me and Sophie from school.

Mrs. Peepers was nothing like Marcy, Linnie's babysitter. Marcy was in high school. Mrs. Peepers was older than old. Definitely older than Mom. Marcy did fun things with Linnie, like play games and put together puzzles. Mrs. Peepers made us do our homework. The only game she played with me and Sophie was the "be very quiet" game. That was not a fun game at all.

Sophie and I walked home with Mrs. Peepers. We didn't talk. We went straight to the kitchen table to do our homework. Mrs. Peepers sat down across from us and took out her knitting.

When I finished my homework, I didn't tell Mrs. Peepers because sometimes she gave me extra work. She carried worksheets in her big knitting bag. I closed my eyes and imagined hitting my taiko. Was it 5, 5, 8 or 5, 5, 3 to start? I squinted hard trying to remember.

I peeked at Mrs. Peepers, who was busy

untangling a knot in her yarn. I peeked at Sophie, who was erasing something on her homework. Under the table, I moved my hands quietly, pretending to hit my taiko, but I couldn't remember the order of my song. I didn't know how I was supposed to practice when Kat couldn't bring my drum until Saturday night at the show. By then, everyone would be better at their talent than me.

I sighed and Sophie looked up at me.

"We're finished with our homework, Mrs. Peepers," Sophie said. "Our mom said we should have reading time in our rooms."

Mrs. Peepers waved her hand and Sophie and I made our escape down the hall to our rooms. I threw myself on my bed and stared up at the ceiling.

"What's with you?" Sophie asked, walking into my room. Sophie said I wasn't allowed to be in her room, but I didn't mind her coming into mine.

"I have no talent," I said, crossing my arms over my face.

"I thought Mom was taking you to taiko lessons?"

I sat up. "She was, but I'm not good. I mess up when I play and I can't remember the order of the song."

"That's what practice is for," Sophie said, leaning against my desk.

"No," I said. "Practice is for when you're not good. If you're talented, you don't need to practice."

"Who said that?"

"Maggie Milsap," I said. "She's the smartest and the best at everything in the third grade."

Sophie flipped her hair over her shoulder. "Well, she's not right about talent. I'm really good at soccer, but we practice twice a week.

It makes me a better soccer player. And for our play, we rehearse our lines every day. Practice is what makes you good."

"Really?"

"Really! Now stop bothering me. I'm going to go read," Sophie said, and she left my room.

I knew Sophie didn't mean it about me bothering her. *She* was the one who came to *my* room. I thought about what she had said about practicing. Sophie is older than Maggie. Sophie is smart. Sophie is also talented, and she needed to practice.

I would practice, too!

PRACTICE MAKES PERFECT

I took out the bachi from under my bed. I closed my eyes. I needed to remember my song. Kat said I had a good memory. I gripped my bachi and took a deep breath:

5, 5, 8, 5, 3, 3, 5, big 8.

My eyes flew open and I grinned. I remembered my song! I hopped and jumped around my room, waving the bachi.

I used my bed as my taiko: 1, 2, 3, 4, 5, HA! The sticks bounced off my bed, which was kind of fun. But it wasn't as exciting as when I hit the drum and it made a big sound.

When I got to the last part, the Big Eight, I remembered that Kat had said I could make up my own pose.

I raised my arms and crossed my sticks and yelled, "SAH!" That felt okay, but it wasn't perfect. I tried again. I jumped with my legs together and pointed the sticks forward and shouted, "SAH!" No, that wasn't it either.

I looked around my room and saw my flamingo collage. Of course!

I hit my bed with my bachi and played my song. When I got to the end, I held my arms out like I had wings and I bent one leg like a flamingo and yelled, "SAH!"

Wowee zowee! That was it!

Then I heard one of the best sounds in the world: the sound of Mom's car pulling up! I ran to the back door and flung it open.

"Mom!" I waved to her. She waved back as she stepped out of the car. Instead of coming to the door, she went to the trunk and took out a big rubber trash can.

"What's that?" I asked.

"A surprise for after dinner," Mom said, dragging the trash can to the garage, where it definitely belonged.

I loved surprises!

* * *

After dinner, Mom asked the entire family to come to the garage. Mom dragged the rubber trash can into the driveway.

"It's upside down," I said.

"And what's with all the tape on it?" Sophie asked.

Strips of clear tape crisscrossed the bottom. Green and red tape circled the sides.

"Hey," I said. "It kind of looks like a big taiko drum."

Mom grinned. "It is! It's a gomi-kan, or a trash-can taiko. You can use this to practice and for the dress rehearsal," Mom said. "Do you want to try it now?"

"Hai!" I shouted *yes*. I ran to my room and grabbed my bachi.

When I got back outside, Mom, Dad, and Sophie were sitting in folding chairs from the garage. I walked to the gomi-kan. My first performance.

I stood at rest position, and then jumped into ready.

Dad started clapping.

"Not yet," I said, grinning.

Sophie rolled her eyes. She thought Dad was silly, with his lame dad jokes. I thought Dad was funny.

I took a deep breath. Then I started playing. The gomi-kan made an odd sound, a muffled *boom*, and my sticks were bouncier off this drum, but it was still a drum!

Boom, boom, boom, boom, boom. "HA!" I shouted. I went through my whole song with no mistakes. I did my big finish in my Super Jasmine Drummer Girl Flamingo Pose, both sticks held out while I balanced on one leg. I yelled, "SAH!"

Mom, Dad, and even Sophie cheered.

I had done it! Wait till Maggie Milsap saw my taiko performance. She wasn't the only one with talent!

DRESS REHEARSAL

Friday was dress rehearsal day. After morning math time, we walked to the auditorium, where we would watch the practice talent show. The seats in the auditorium squeaked and creaked as students fidgeted from nerves and excitement.

I sat through the kindergartners singing the teapot song. They were very cute. The first graders sang a song, too, but they also did it in sign language. That was pretty cool. Now the

second graders were on the stage. Two girls bounced a soccer ball back and forth. Then a boy did a gymnastics tumbling act. While the second graders were doing their talents, Ms. Sanchez led our class out of our rows and backstage, where we lined up in order.

Maggie was third and I was last. Maggie probably thought that made her better than me. It didn't matter. I was going to be great!

I held my bachi in my left hand. Kat said taiko was about respect. Respect for space, the equipment, and people, including myself. That meant not goofing off with the drum or bachi, or swinging the bachi around at others. It also meant enjoying myself. I didn't usually like rules, but I liked taiko so much that I even liked its rules.

When it was our class's turn, I tried to peek over the line of my classmates. I couldn't see, but I heard Maggie Milsap's violin. I hated to admit it, but she sounded good. The music floated through the air. She didn't make any mistakes.

One by one, my classmates performed their talents onstage, and one by one they returned to their seats in the audience. By the time it was Linnie's turn, I could see the stage. Whoa. That stage was pretty big. Linnie sat at Mr. Peters's music-class piano and started playing. Linnie was awesome. When she was done, I clapped and cheered for her. She looked back at me and smiled as she curtsied to the audience.

It was almost my turn. The fourth graders lined up behind me, waiting for our class to finish.

Every single one of my classmates had done a great job. It was hard to tell who was the best, though. Maggie was good, but so were Linnie and Daisy and everyone else. I wanted to be the best, too.

"And next is Jasmine Toguchi, who will play the Japanese taiko," Mrs. Tasker said, her voice echoing through the big auditorium.

I walked onto the stage. It felt

huge. Ms. Sanchez brought out my gomi-kan and I heard Maggie Milsap say, "Is that a trash can?"

Some people laughed. My face flamed up.

Mrs. Tasker stepped onto the stage from behind the curtains. She didn't say anything, but she looked out into the audience and the laughter quieted. My hands felt sweaty and my throat got tight. I looked out into the audience, too. There were so many people! I hadn't realized how many kids went to our school. Millions!

I stood at rest position and then jumped into ready, holding the bachi over the gomi-kan. I counted aloud, "Ichi, ni, san, SO-RE!"

I lifted my right hand and the bachi flew out of my sweaty grip. A few students snickered. I nibbled my bottom lip and walked over to retrieve my stick. I curled my hands around the sticks with my thumbs wrapped tight, but not too tight. I stood at the gomi-kan again.

The whole auditorium was full of squeaks and creaks and whispers. I looked into the audience. Linnie nodded at me.

I started again. I hit the gomi-kan. Five hits and I shouted, "HA!" That made everyone stop

rustling around. I hit it again five times and shouted, "HA!" Then I hit it eight times — and that was when my mind went blank. I shouted, "HA!" again but I knew that wasn't right. The rest of the song flew right out of my head. I froze and then everyone started clapping like they thought that was the end of the song. I didn't know what to do, so I bowed and walked off the stage, blinking back tears.

I could hardly watch the rest of the talent show. Everyone was better than me. Sophie's class was the last performance. It was a really good play, and it almost made me forget about my horrible performance. Almost. Not quite.

It didn't make Maggie Milsap forget either. When we walked back to our classroom, Maggie was right behind me.

"I was the best of all," Maggie said loudly.

"You were wonderful, Jasmine," Linnie said, and she squeezed my hand.

I was pretty sure Maggie was right.

TALENT-SHOW TiME!

At home after dinner on Friday, I practiced and practiced on the gomi-kan. I practiced until my throat was sore from HA-ing and SO-RE-ing. I practiced until my arms felt like rubber bands. I chanted "5, 5, 8, 5, 3, 3, 5, big 8" until it was like breathing.

"Jasmine," Mom said, walking up to me in front of the garage. "I think you've practiced enough. In fact, I've never seen such dedication."

"I'm not ready," I said, breathing like I had run around the block a hundred times. I held the bachi at my side in resting position.

"Yes, you are," Mom said. "I've been watching you from the kitchen window. You're really good!"

"I messed up at dress rehearsal," I said, my shoulders drooping. "I dropped the bachi and I didn't even finish the song."

Mom took my wobbly arm and pulled me over to the stuffed chair in the garage to sit down. "Sometimes we make mistakes, but nobody will know if you just carry on."

"I'll know. You'll know. Kat will know."

"So what?" Mom said.

That surprised me. Mom never said things like "So what." "I'll be embarrassed," I said.

"Nobody ever died from embarrassment," Mom said. "I'll be proud of you just for being on that stage. Now get ready for bed. Tomorrow is a long day."

The next afternoon we had to go to Sophie's soccer game. I wouldn't get to practice again. I followed Mom into the house and glanced sadly back at the gomi-kan, wishing I could practice all night long.

* * *

On Saturday night, my family drove to Drake Elementary. The school was lit up like a party. I'd never seen it at night before. Cars were crammed into the parking lot and along the street.

"Are you sure Kat is coming?" I asked for the hundredth time.

"Yes, Jasmine," Mom said. "Please calm down."

Inside the auditorium, it sounded like ocean waves. Voices mixed with the sound of feet and dragging equipment, roaring like the sea.

My parents gave me and Sophie hugs and

told us we'd be great. As
Dad hugged me, I saw
Maggie. A man and a lady,
probably her parents, hur-
ried over to her. Maggie's
dad was tapping on his

phone with a frown on his face. Maggie's mom
handed her a violin case and then chased after
twin boys who must have been Maggie's little
brothers. And then Maggie was standing
by herself.

Maggie looked up and saw me
watching her. She glared at me and

walked away toward the stage. I shrugged and followed her to where the rest of my class was supposed to meet.

Backstage, I found Linnie, who wore a silvery dress with a green bow.

"You look very pretty," I said to her.

"Thanks," she said. "So do you."

I was wearing a long sparkly purple shirt and black leggings. I felt like a purple flamingo.

The lights flickered and the roar in the auditorium faded to a hush.

Mrs. Tasker stepped onto the stage. "Thank you for coming, friends and families of Drake Elementary. All the students worked hard, and I hope you'll enjoy the show!"

The kindergartners sang their teapot song. The first graders did their sign language song. Before I knew it, we were lined up near the stage waiting for our turn.

"Are you ready?" Kat stepped up next to me.

My heart thumped louder than a taiko drum, even though I was happy to see her.

"I don't think I can do it," I said in a shivery whisper.

"I know you can," Kat said. "Remember, it's not about being perfect, it's about having fun. Do you have fun playing taiko?"

I closed my eyes. Hitting the taiko made me feel strong. I loved the big sound of the drum. Every time I played, I had fun! I was excited to play the hira-daiko again. I nodded.

"Then that's all that matters," Kat said. She held up a rectangular piece of cloth. "Your mom told me that purple is your favorite color."

I nodded again. The fabric was white with pretty purple flowers.

"This is a hachi-maki," Kat said. She folded the rectangle twice and then twisted it until it was a long roll. She wrapped it around my forehead. "The hachi-maki keeps sweat from rolling into your eyes. It also symbolizes courage. It's like a badge to show strength."

The hachi-maki sat like a crown around my head. It made me feel braver.

And then it was our class's turn.

A MIRACLE

I stood on tiptoe. Maggie Milsap walked onto the stage with her violin.

She started playing, the melody drifting up and out over the audience. Suddenly a screech came from the violin. I pushed my way forward. Maggie was frozen on the stage, her wide eyes staring in shock at her violin. She ran her bow across the strings again. It screeched again. Maggie dropped the bow onto the stage and her cheeks turned bright pink. The audience rustled in their seats.

Maggie Milsap stood there for what felt like forever until Ms. Sanchez went onstage while clapping. The audience clapped, too, but it was a polite clap, not a cheering type of clap. Ms. Sanchez picked up the bow and guided Maggie off the stage and then Tommy walked on with his yo-yo.

I thought I would feel happy seeing Maggie mess up, but I felt bad for her. She hadn't kept playing, like Mom said I should if I messed up. I couldn't believe Maggie hadn't had a perfect performance! Everything about Maggie was perfect.

When it was finally my turn, Kat stepped onto the stage and set up my hira-daiko. My stomach dipped. I'd been practicing first on air, then on my bed, and then on the gomi-kan. What if I couldn't play the hira-daiko anymore? If perfect, talented Maggie messed up, how could I, with my brand-new talent, play without mistakes?

There was no more time to worry. I walked onto the stage, squinting into the bright light. I remembered playing at Kat's house. I remembered playing on the gomi-kan. I touched my hachi-maki for good luck. Then I took a deep breath.

"Ichi, ni, san, SO-RE," I said with a little tremble in my voice.

I hit the hira-daiko.

Boom, boom, boom, boom, boom!

I raised my arms and shouted, "HA!"

I hit the drum again five times and shouted, "HA!" once more.

My arms were strong. My voice was loud. My heart lifted. This was fun!

Without worrying or thinking, I kept playing. The drum boomed! My voice boomed! I played without any mistakes! I didn't drop the sticks and I yelled all the right sounds at all the right times.

I hit the drum eight times slowly for the Big Eight.

Boom, boom, boom, boom, boom, boom, boom, boom!

Then I went into my Super Jasmine Drummer Girl Flamingo Pose. I held out my sticks and lifted my arms like they were wings, and I stood on one leg and yelled, "SAH!"

The audience clapped and I grinned. I bowed and walked off the stage.

When I sat down backstage, Linnie leaned over and gave me a big hug. "You did it, Jasmine!" she said, smiling. Tommy and Daisy waved to me. I sat back in my chair, joy and relief bubbling inside me.

I looked around and saw Maggie sitting by herself next to the exit door. Her hair hung down over her face and her shoulders slumped forward. My chest tightened.

I walked over to her, and when she saw me standing next to her, she made a face. "What do you want?" she asked, her eyes looking nervous.

"I thought you did a good job," I said.

"Are you trying to be funny?" she asked.

I shook my head. "The violin looks hard."

"It is." Maggie clasped her hands together. "The best I've ever played it was at dress rehearsal, actually."

"The song was pretty," I said.

Maggie looked down at her shiny black shoes. "It doesn't matter. I didn't play it perfectly.

Now my parents won't take me to get a hamburger and my favorite strawberry milk-shake."

"Don't you like playing the violin?" I asked.

Maggie shrugged. "It's okay."

"I love playing taiko," I said.

"It does look fun," Maggie said.

Maggie's voice sounded different. Normally she was so loud. Normally I tried not to listen to her. But this was not a normally time. I remembered what Ms. Sanchez had said about being friendly to Maggie because she was new and didn't have friends here yet.

"Maybe you can take taiko lessons, too," I said, surprising both me and Maggie. "Maybe you can come with me to my next lesson."

"Really?" Maggie said, smiling. "That would be cool!"

I smiled back. Already she sounded more like herself.

"I'm sorry for saying you wouldn't be the best," she said. "You did a great job."

"Thanks!" I said. "I think you did, too. We *tried* our best."

I thought about how awesome taiko sounded when Kat and I played at the same time. If Maggie and I played together, that was how we'd sound. *Wowee zowee!*

Maybe the real miracle wasn't that I did a great job at the show or that I did better than Maggie. Maybe the miracle was figuring out that it was more important to have fun. And I, Jasmine Toguchi, *love* having fun!

AUTHOR'S NOTE

Taiko means drum in Japanese. The word refers to all types of Japanese drums. Taiko as an instrument has probably been around for thousands of years, used during times of war to motivate and energize troops, in temples and shrines during worship, and in theater for dances and songs. However, playing different taiko together in performance groups is a more modern development, starting in the 1950s.

Taiko are traditionally crafted from a single

piece of wood, carved to be hollow, and covered with animal skin stretched tightly across the top. Making one is a very long process requiring great skill. Today's taiko can also be fashioned out of wooden slats or barrels.

Taiko come in different sizes and have different names, like the medium-size barrel-shaped drum, called the nagado-daiko, and the smaller drum that Jasmine plays, the hira-daiko.

The sticks used to hit taiko are called bachi. In Japan, they are typically made from Japanese white oak, cypress, or magnolia. In the United States, bachi are usually made from maple. Different weights of bachi produce different sounds. Bachi also come in various lengths, and choosing the length of the bachi is a personal preference that might depend on the length of the drummer's arms.

When Jasmine learns to play her taiko song, she learns by counting out the beats. In taiko groups, people usually learn by a method called kuchi-shoga, or mouth song. The players call out the sounds, like DON for long hits and DOKO for short hits.

There are many taiko performance groups across the United States. Maybe you will have a chance to see a performance, which is truly unforgettable. Or maybe you will get a chance to learn to play, just like Jasmine!

MAKE YOUR OWN
HACHI-MAKI

A hachi-maki is a headband worn to catch sweat and keep it from running into your eyes. In Japan, it is also worn to show effort or perseverance during activity.

MATERIALS

- Fabric markers
- A lightweight piece of cloth, cut ahead of time by an adult into a long rectangle (approximately 30 × 10 inches)

INSTRUCTIONS

1. Use the fabric markers to draw on and decorate the cloth.

2. Lay the cloth down flat, lengthwise, with the pattern side down.

3. Fold the bottom side about a third of the way up.

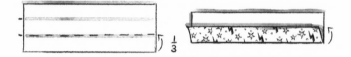

4. Fold the top side about a third of the way down, over the section that you folded up. Now you have a long, skinny rectangle/band.

5. Take one end in each hand and twist the fabric until you have a long roll. Hold on to the ends so the roll doesn't untwist.

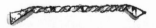

For these next steps, you might need someone to help you.

6. Wrap the hachi-maki around your head, above your eyes.

7. Take the ends and twist them around each other (do not tie them) at the back of your head.

8. After you twist the ends around each other, tuck each end up under the band to secure it.

You are now wearing a hachi-maki!

Turn the page for a sneak peek of . . .

Coming soon!

SATURDAY FUN DAY

I, Jasmine Toguchi, love Saturdays because Saturdays are super-fun days. Sometimes we have family time, when Dad, Mom, my sister, and I go to the zoo or the movies. Sometimes I play in my neighbor Mrs. Reese's garage. On this Saturday I got to have lunch with my best friend, Linnie Green, at her house.

"Jasmine, are you ready?" Mom called to me from the living room.

No, I was not ready. I was looking for my

special rock. Linnie collects rocks, and she gave me her favorite pink rock because it looks like a flamingo egg. Flamingos are my very favorite animal in the world. I wanted to bring the rock with me so she could see it again. I looked on my desk, but it wasn't there. I looked under my bed, but it wasn't there either.

"Why are you in your closet?" My big sister, Sophie, poked her head into my room. "If you don't get in the car right now, you're going to make me late for my soccer game."

"Walnuts! I can't find my rock," I said.

"Maybe you should check your head," Sophie said, and laughed. This was her way of joking, even if it wasn't very funny.

Ever since Sophie started fifth grade, she seemed to get bossier every day. Sophie was always telling me what I couldn't do. Like, go into her room or touch her things. Sometimes I wondered if I had done something to make her mad at me. Or maybe she just didn't like me anymore. That made my chest feel tight and sad. But even having her say not-funny jokes to me was better than feeling invisible.

"Ha-ha," I said.

"Jasmine Toguchi," Mom shouted. "We're going to be late!"

"Hurry up!" Sophie said.

I took one last look around my bedroom and then ran after my sister. My flamingo-egg rock would have to stay behind.

✦ ✦ ✦

"You're here!" Linnie shouted as she flung open her front door.

I turned to wave at my parents, and they drove off to take Sophie to her soccer game. I followed Linnie into her house.

There was a little blanket in the middle of the living room. That was different. Linnie is very neat and never leaves things lying around. Then we walked through to the kitchen.

"What's that?" I asked, pointing to a bowl of water on the floor. Mrs. Green is also very neat. She doesn't even leave her cooking things out on the counter, so it was strange that she would leave something on the floor.

"A surprise," Linnie said, giggling.

I like a good surprise, but I wasn't sure about this one. What if the surprise was that we were going to clean up? Or maybe eat lunch on the floor? Actually, that might not be so bad. It could be fun, like a picnic. I hoped the surprise was a picnic and not cleaning. I am *not* a fan of cleaning.

I have been to Linnie's house a million times, so it feels like a second home to me. I walked down the hall to her bedroom because that's what we always do. We always go to her room for her special suitcase that's filled with a bunch of old Halloween costumes. We play dress up and pretend we are princesses, ballerinas, knights, and bunnies. But Linnie didn't follow me.

"Where are you?" I called out.

"Over here," she said, laughing. "Come this way!"

Linnie stood at the sliding glass door to the backyard. This surprised me since Linnie doesn't like playing outside. She is afraid of dirt and heights and bugs. Okay, maybe not *afraid*. But she doesn't like those things as much as I do. Linnie is trying to be braver these days. Maybe this was her surprise, that we were going to play outside!

Linnie held a tennis ball. Were we going to play catch? I didn't really *love* to play catch. It was boring throwing a ball back and forth, but because Linnie is my very best friend in the world, I am happy to do things that she likes to do.

Linnie opened the sliding door, and I followed her into the yard. And that's when I heard a strange sound.

LINNIE'S SURPRISE

"Woof!"

Before I could ask Linnie what that sound was, a little black-and-white dog galloped toward us.

"Wowee zowee, Linnie!" I said. "Is that a puppy?"

Linnie sat down and the dog scrambled over and licked Linnie's face. "Sure is," she said. "And she's *my* puppy! Her name is Trixie."

I sat down next to Linnie on the grass and

the puppy leaped into my lap and started licking my face, too. It tickled and I laughed. But I closed my lips quickly, because as much as I liked dog kisses, I did *not* want dog slobber in my mouth!

Linnie threw the ball across the yard. Trixie ran after it.

"My parents finally got me a dog," Linnie said with a huge smile. "I've been asking for one for a long time!"

"You're so lucky," I said.

Trixie bounded back over with the ball in her mouth. Linnie took the ball and threw it

for her puppy again. Now I knew why there was a bowl on the kitchen floor and a blanket in the living room. They were for Trixie.

As we played fetch, the ball got wetter and wetter with dog slobber, but I didn't mind. I just wiped it off onto my jeans.

"Trixie is so cute with her black spot and waggy tail," I said. "How did you convince your parents to get you a dog?" Maybe I could try some of Linnie's tricks to convince *my* parents to get me a pet flamingo, even though Mom says flamingos belong in the wild.

"I had to show my mom and dad that I was responsible enough to take care of a pet. That means I had to take care of myself without being told, like keeping my room clean, brushing my teeth, and clearing the table after meals."

That sounded like a lot of work.

"I also showed them how much I knew about taking care of a dog, like feeding it and taking it for walks. I read a lot of books about dogs."

I liked to read.

"The truth is," Linnie said with a smile, "my mom really wanted a dog, too, so it didn't take a lot of convincing."

I was pretty sure I was the only one in my family who wanted a pet flamingo. I would have to work hard to make my parents believe I would be a good flamingo keeper.

* * *

Mom picked me up after lunch.

"Linnie got a puppy named Trixie!" I told her. "She is so soft and fluffy. We played fetch and then we walked her around the block on her leash. Then I got to feed Trixie some dog cookies. She loved those! Linnie is going to teach her tricks like roll over and sit up!"

"It sounds like you two had a lot of fun," Mom said. "I'll bet Linnie's very happy with her new puppy."

"She is," I said. And soon I'd be very happy with my own pet flamingo. I just wasn't sure how to go about getting one yet.

When we pulled into our driveway, Sophie was waiting for us. That was strange. She had changed out of her soccer uniform and into her regular clothes. That was not so strange. As soon as Mom stopped the car and turned off the engine, Sophie ran over to Mom's side and opened her door. That was strange.

Mom must have thought so, too, because when she got out of the car she asked, "Is something wrong?"

"Quick!" Sophie said, and started pulling on Mom's arm.

"What's going on?" Mom asked, tripping as Sophie tugged her toward the house.

I ran after Mom and Sophie. Had Sophie broken something in the house? No, if she had, she wouldn't rush to show Mom. Was Dad hurt? A tickle of worry wiggled its way through me, making my stomach feel funny. I caught up to them just as they walked through the back door into the kitchen.